W9-BZD-076

Christmas in Silver Lake

Treasured Horses Collection™

titles in Large-Print Editions:

Changing Times

Christmas in Silver Lake

Colorado Summer

The Flying Angels

A Horse for Hannah

Kate's Secret Plan

Louisiana Blue

Pretty Lady of Saratoga

Pride of the Green Mountains

Ride of Courage

Riding School Rivals

Rush for Gold

Spirit of the West

The Stallion of Box Canyon

CHRISTMAS IN SILVER LAKE

The story of a dependable Clydesdale and the immigrant girl who turns to her for comfort

Written by Coleen Hubbard
Story by Deborah Felder
Illustrated by Sandy Rabinowitz
Cover Illustration by Christa Keiffer
Developed by Nancy Hall, Inc.

Gareth Stevens Publishing
MILWAUKEE

For a free color catalog describing Gareth Stevens' list of high-quality books and multimedia programs, call 1-800-542-2595 (USA) or 1-800-461-9120 (Canada). Gareth Stevens Publishing's Fax: (414) 225-0377.

Library of Congress Cataloging-in-Publication Data

Hubbard, Coleen.
Christmas in Silver Lake / written by Coleen Hubbard;
illustrated by Sandy Rabinowitz; cover illustration by Christa Keiffer.
p. cm.
Originally published: Dyersville, Iowa: Ertl Co., 1997.
(Treasured horses collection)
Summary: Eleven-year-old Erika has difficulty adjusting to life in Minnesota
when her family moves there from Germany in 1880, but a special
Clydesdale horse not only helps her fit in, but also saves her life.
ISBN 0-8368-2400-8 (lib. bdg.)
[1. Immigrants—Fiction. 2. German Americans—Fiction.
3. Clydesdale horse—Fiction. 4. Horses—Fiction.]
I. Rabinowitz, Sandy, ill. II. Title.
III. Series: Treasured horses collection.
PZ7.H85668Ch 1999
[Fic]—dc21 99-11768

This edition first published in 1999 by
Gareth Stevens Publishing
1555 North RiverCenter Drive, Suite 201
Milwaukee, Wisconsin 53212 USA

First published by The ERTL Company, Inc., Dyersville, Iowa.

Printed in the United States of America

1 2 3 4 5 6 7 8 9 03 02 01 00 99

CONTENTS

"In English, Please!"

"W*hat is the date?"* Erika Meyer asked herself in German as she walked toward the barn. "It is October 10, Saturday, 1880," she answered. She was certain that her English wasn't exactly right, but she knew she had to keep trying.

"How old are you?" she continued in German. And again she answered in the broken English of one learning a new and difficult language. "I are—I am—eleven."

Inside the barn, Erika busied herself with her least favorite chore—grooming her family's Clydesdale horse, Silky. Silky was enormous, standing nearly seventeen hands high. To brush Silky's broad back,

Erika had to stand on a stool.

As Erika carefully brushed the mare, she continued to quiz herself in German and answer in English.

"How long have you lived in Silver Lake, Minnesota?" she asked. This was a hard one. She had to concentrate on how to compose her answer, because it had two parts. Her papa, Karl Meyer, had moved from their hometown in Germany the year before to set up their new home, but Erika had just made the long journey with her mama and five-year-old sister, Lise, in May. "Five months only," she finally answered.

Erika felt the now familiar wave of homesickness rise up in her. It made her eyes sting with tears and her throat close tight. It happened every day, and Erika knew it was no coincidence that she always felt the worst when she was alone in the barn with Silky.

"Please stand still!" she told Silky impatiently.

Silky turned her handsome face with its gentle eyes toward Erika. She nickered a friendly greeting and stood quietly. "Ah, good," Erika said, kneeling down to comb Silky's feathers. Papa had named the Clydesdale after her feathers—the long, silky hair that flowed down around her legs and over her hooves.

Erika combed out a tangle. *"I know you can't help it,"* she said to the horse. *"But I already have a horse, a horse I love. Her name is Starlight, and she's living with my cousins in Germany. She's beautiful–deep black, with a white star marking on her forehead. She's fast and sleek, and we rode every day. She's the only horse for me!"*

"Say it in English, please!" boomed Erika's father. He stood in the barn door, his arms crossed over his large chest. His decades of working as a builder and carpenter had chiseled his body into hard muscles. Like Erika's younger sister, Papa had curly blond hair and deep blue eyes. Erika favored her mother, with wavy dark hair and eyes that flashed tints of blue and green.

"I can't say that much in English," Erika protested. *"You know I'm still learning."*

"The only way to learn, Erika, is to speak always English. Even to the horse."

"But Papa," Erika pleaded. *"It's hard! Why must I not speak German? I AM GERMAN!"*

To make himself understood, Papa forgot his own rule. *"You are German, of course, sweet child. But we are Americans now. We live in America. We're starting our life over, with so much more opportunity, and we have to speak the language."*

Erika nodded. She loved her papa, and she knew he was trying to help. But he didn't understand anything! He didn't understand how homesick she was, how she longed for her old home and school and friends! He couldn't possibly understand how much she missed Starlight and how much she disliked Silky.

Papa had surprised Erika with Silky her first day on the farm. He had been so excited, thinking the horse would make up for all Erika had left behind. Instead the moment she saw the large, muscled work horse she had burst into tears. Silky was so different from Starlight—as different as Germany was from America.

Still Erika took good care of the horse. She understood that without Silky, Papa wouldn't be able to plow the fields or carry heavy loads. Deep down she knew Papa was right when he told her that Silky was the kind of horse they needed for their new life in America.

Papa moved next to her and patted her shoulder. "Silky looks beautiful, Erika. You did a fine job grooming her."

"Thank you," she said in English. But in German she added, *"I don't know what good it will do. Those feathery legs will just get muddy and tangled the minute we leave the barn."*

Just then Lise burst into the barn, out of breath

with excitement. *"Hurry! Hurry! It's time to go to the Harvest Festival. Mama is all ready, and I'm ready too!"*

Lise was always spilling over with enthusiasm and laughter. To Erika, it seemed as if her little sister was never unhappy.

"I'll hitch up Silky," Papa said. "Help your mama with the food."

Erika pulled her sweater from the hook on the barn door and exchanged her wooden shoes for short leather boots. She tried to smooth the wild curls that escaped from her careful braids. Then she joined Mama who was walking toward the wagon with two large baskets of food.

"At least I have the festival to look forward to," she whispered to herself.

The Harvest Festival in Silver Lake would be her first celebration in America. All summer she had been busy helping Mama with the housework and Papa with the planting. She'd only visited the town once with Papa, to buy supplies at Per Andersson's General Store. There she'd seen several girls who looked to be her age, but she'd been too shy to speak to them.

"Maybe today I'll meet some friends. I could certainly use a friend before I start school tomorrow," Erika said to Mama.

Erika and Mama settled the baskets into the back

of the wagon and folded an old quilt over them.

"I know you'll have friends," Mama replied, pulling herself up to the wagon seat. *"At home you had many friends because you're a friendly person and you have a beautiful smile!"* Mama always knew how to soothe Erika, and she never said a word about speaking English. She just went about her work, singing to herself in German, stopping when one of her daughters needed a hug or a word of encouragement.

Erika settled herself in the back of the wagon with Lise. Papa slapped Silky's reins, but the Clydesdale didn't budge.

"She likes it when you say, 'Hup!'" Erika told Papa.

"In English, please!" Papa said.

"Hup!" Erika hollered, laughing at Papa. *Hup* wasn't a word in German or English. It was just a shout to get Silky going.

"Hup!" Papa hollered, and Silky moved forward, using her weight and strength to smoothly pull the heavy wagon and four eager passengers.

"Silky likes you best," Papa called back to Erika. "You and she are a good team. She likes it when you drive the wagon."

Erika knew that what he said was true. She and Silky did make a good team. She wondered, though, how it was possible that Silky liked and trusted her, when she didn't care much at all for Silky.

While Lise played with her beloved doll Gretel, Erika studied the landscape around her. To the north was a forest of pine trees and the small lake that had given the town of Silver Lake its name. Far to the east were the cities of Minneapolis and St. Paul. West was the Dakota Territory, and between east and west stretched hundreds of miles of rolling, grassy, American prairie.

Erika wondered if she would ever get used to the wide open spaces of her new country. In Germany she had lived in a busy village, close to her cousins and friends. She had walked to school and to the shops. Here, on the farm, she felt both alone and lonely.

Suddenly, Erika's mother shouted and pointed. *"Look, Karl! Look at that wagon up ahead. They've had an accident!"*

Sure enough, Erika spotted a wagon turned over on its side in a ditch. A woman and two girls stood beside it, waving at the Meyers as they approached.

"Do you know them, Karl?" Mama asked.

"It's Anna Lindstrom and her daughters. I helped her husband, Sven, build his new barn when I first arrived here." Papa brought the wagon to a stop beside them. "Hello," he called out in English.

"Hello, hello, hello!" Lise repeated happily.

"Oh, Mr. Meyer! We're so happy to see you," Mrs. Lindstrom said. She spoke in careful English, but Erika could tell from her accent that she was Swedish. "We were on the way to the festival when we broke a wheel."

"Are you hurt?" Papa asked.

"We're fine, thank you. But we're a little bit—stuck!" Mrs. Lindstrom laughed. She was short and round, and her laugh poured out of her like rushing water. The younger of the two girls, who looked to be about eight, smiled up at Lise and Erika. But the older girl, closer to Erika's own age, stood silently by her mother, looking down the road. Both girls wore their shiny blonde hair in braided loops on either side of their head.

"We would be happy to take you with us," Papa said. "I'll tie your horse to the back of our wagon."

"Oh, you have saved us!" Mrs. Lindstrom said. "Sven is meeting us at the festival. He will be so grateful!"

Erika didn't understand all that Mrs. Lindstrom said, but she sounded friendly. *"This could be it,"* Erika said to Mama, looking at the older Lindstrom girl. *"This could be my new friend!"*

Papa helped Mrs. Lindstrom and her daughters

into the back of the wagon. Then they all began a complicated round of introductions.

"I'm Anna Lindstrom," she told Mama in English. "My younger daughter is Inger, and my oldest is Kari."

"Pleased to meet you," Mama said in German. *"My name is Frieda Meyer."*

"Good day, Mrs. Meyer," the Lindstrom girls answered in English.

"This is Erika, our oldest," Papa said, pointing at Erika. "And the little one is Lise."

"Hello, hello!" Lise said. The only English word she seemed to know was *hello*, and she never grew tired of saying it.

"Good day to you," Erika said, trying to imitate Kari's careful pronunciation.

"How long have you been here?" Kari asked Erika. "Are you going to school? Where do you live?"

Erika panicked. She hadn't expected Kari to speak English so well, and her rapid-fire questions threw Erika into a confused silence. *"Help me, Papa,"* she whispered.

Papa translated Kari's questions and Erika's answers, but it didn't feel much like a conversation. Kari seemed very impatient.

"Are you going to enter the wagon-pulling contest at the festival?" Kari asked.

Erika shrugged helplessly, until Papa translated.

"I enter every year," Kari continued. "With our Shire, Max. Papa's driving him to the festival right now. He looks like your horse, except he's much stronger. We always win the contest. We're the best team in Silver Lake."

"Now don't boast, Kari," Mrs. Lindstrom said to her daughter.

"Well, it's true," Kari insisted. "We always win."

Again Papa translated, but Erika could only say, "Silky is a good horse."

Papa explained to Kari that Erika had been in Silver Lake for only five months and that she was still learning English. He added that Erika was an excellent horse driver, and that maybe she and Silky would enter the contest.

Hearing that, Kari suddenly frowned hard at Erika. Erika had no idea why, since she hadn't understood the previous exchange.

"Did I say something wrong, Papa?" Erika asked. *"Is she mad at me?"*

Papa shook his head. *"Be patient, Erika,"* he said. *"New friendships take time."*

Erika sighed and looked over at Kari. She tried to smile at her, but Kari and Inger were speaking Swedish to each other.

Erika felt left out. Her parents spoke softly to each other in German while the Lindstrom girls laughed and joked in Swedish. Mrs. Lindstrom and Lise were playing a wordless game with Lise's doll.

I guess that leaves me with Silky, Erika thought sadly. *My only friend here is a horse I don't like who doesn't speak any language at all!*

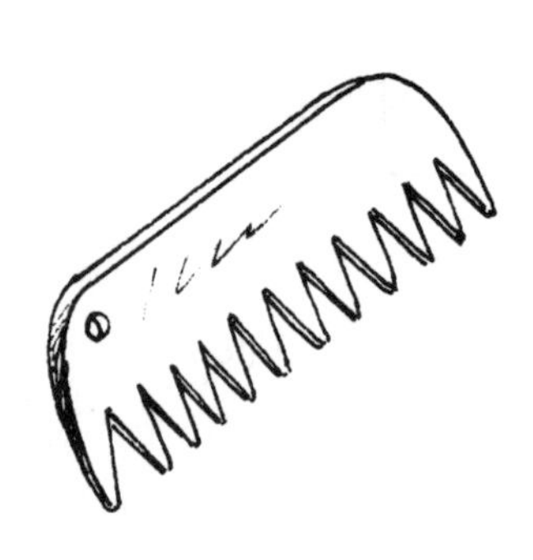

The Harvest Festival

"There it is!" Lise cried, grabbing Erika's arm. "There's the town! See the church?"

Sure enough, the town of Silver Lake came into view as Silky pulled the loaded wagon down the dirt road.

"Do you see it, Erika?" Lise asked again, practically jumping out of the wagon.

"I've been to town with Papa, remember?" Erika told her sister. She couldn't blame Lise for being excited. It was Lise's first time off the farm since they'd arrived in America. And Lise loved large gatherings. She always sparkled in a crowd.

Erika glanced over at Kari and Inger, but they

were deep in conversation with their mother, speaking in Swedish. She longed to be able to join their discussion.

Soon Papa turned onto Main Street, and they passed by houses and shops and the school where Erika would begin lessons the following day. Just looking at the schoolhouse made Erika's stomach churn. She wondered what the teacher would be like and if she would be able to understand anything at all.

"There's the festival!" Lise shouted. *"Look at all the people!"*

Mama turned and smiled at her daughters, pinning a stray curl back in place. *"You've been so quiet, Erika,"* she said. *"How are you feeling?"*

"I'm fine, Mama," Erika assured her. *"Just thinking."*

"Promise me you'll stop thinking so much and have a good time at the festival. Yes? A promise?"

Erika smiled at her mother. *"I promise. But no one will have as much fun as Lise."* They shared a laugh at that, and Lise threw her hands high over her head in agreement.

Papa stopped behind the church at the field, which was filled with wagons just like theirs. All around them families busily tended to their horses and unloaded their baskets of food. Kari immediately jumped out of the wagon and started to run toward the long tables covered with bright cloths.

"Kari, come back here!" Mrs. Lindstrom commanded. "Please don't be rude. You must thank Mr. and Mrs. Meyer."

Kari returned and stood by her mother. "Thank you, Mr. Meyer," she said. "Thank you, Mrs. Meyer."

"You are most welcome," Papa replied. "Always we are glad to help."

Kari and Inger disappeared into the crowd. Mrs. Lindstrom thanked Papa and Mama over and over, using her careful English sprinkled with a few Swedish words. "Please sit with my family," she said. "We would be honored."

Papa translated and Mama nodded happily, glad for the invitation. Erika and Mama followed Mrs. Lindstrom, each of them carrying a basket of food. Lise ran happily ahead, waving her doll in her outstretched hand.

"Why don't you go play?" Mama asked Erika. *"I can set the food out by myself."* She arranged bread and butter, potato salad, pickles, corn salad, and a beautiful plum cake on her own embroidered linen cloth. The sight of the food made Erika weak with hunger, so she took a thick slice of the braided loaf of bread and gave Mama a quick hug.

"Go!" her mother said, pretending to swat at Erika.

Erika looked around at the crowd. Groups of people mingled and talked, laughed and shouted, enjoying the chance to be together and share the rewards of their harvest. She spotted Lise chasing after a little boy who teasingly had grabbed her doll. In a clearing beneath a clump of trees, Erika watched as Kari and several friends braided each other's hair.

They look like they're having so much fun! Erika thought. She remembered the hours she used to spend with her own friends in Germany—braiding hair, sketching pictures, throwing stones into a nearby pond, dreaming about their future.

Erika turned away from the girls and went to find her family's wagon. Maybe she would pretend to busy herself with Silky, and then no one would know that she didn't yet have the courage to approach people in her new, strange country.

Silky was hitched to a post, next to the Lindstrom's mare. Erika watched as the horses touched noses in a friendly way. *"Even you have a friend,"* Erika said to Silky. *"It must be nice to be a horse. You can make friends without talking."*

Silky snorted playfully at Erika and moved toward her. Erika reached out to stroke Silky's side. Erika felt a pang of regret that she paid so little attention to Silky. But it was so hard! She couldn't stop thinking of Starlight. Silky wasn't the kind of horse you took out for a fast, exciting ride. Silky was a work horse—proud and strong and patient—but not the kind of horse a girl became attached to.

"What adventures could the two of us possibly have together?" Erika said, trying to smooth some tangled hair in Silky's mane.

"In English, please!" Papa said, coming up behind her.

"Papa!" Erika exclaimed. *"You scared me."*

"It's time for supper," Papa said. "Pastor Bergman must—is wanting to begin the prayer." Papa put his two hands together, as if he were praying, to give Erika a hint about the English words.

"To pray?"

"Yes!" Papa said. "That's right."

"And—to eat?" Erika asked.

"Good! Yes, it's time to eat. Come!"

Erika took Papa's hand and walked with him to the tables. They squeezed in next to Lise and Mama, just as Pastor Bergman raised his hand for silence.

The tall, white haired man, speaking in English, asked everyone to join hands and bow their heads. In a warm voice he said, "We thank You for the bounty of our harvest and for our friends and families gathered together. We recognize the wonder of our land and all that we can accomplish when we work together and take care of each other."

Erika missed most of the words, but she felt the spirit of joy behind them. She felt safe and protected sitting beside her parents and her sister, with all the wonderful food in front of them.

Later, after the meal, a burly man with a bald head and a long brown beard approached Papa. He clapped Papa on the back and shook his hand. "I can't thank you enough," he said, "for giving my wife and daughters a ride, neighbor."

Papa stood up and smiled. "Always I am glad to help," he said. "I would like you to meet my wife and my daughters. This is Mr. Lindstrom."

Mr. Lindstrom winked at Erika. Papa told her to introduce herself. "I am Erika Meyer," she said. It was one English phrase she was sure of. "This is Lise," she added.

"Very good," Mr. Lindstrom said. "I know it's hard to learn the language. We've been here for three years and I'm still learning. But my daughters—they astound me. Kari speaks like she was born here. Have you met my Kari and Inger?"

Papa translated and Erika smiled and nodded her head. Kari's papa and mama were so friendly. Surely when Kari had the chance to get to know Erika better, she would be friendly, too. Wouldn't she?

Just then the pastor rang a large bell. "It's time," he called out, "for our annual wagon races. We'll start with the children. Any young ladies or gentlemen who would like to enter, please line up your horse and wagon in the north field. Remember, the winner will receive three dollars worth of goods from Mr. Andersson's store."

"Are you going to enter?" Mr. Lindstrom asked Erika. "That horse of yours looks exceptionally strong."

"Are you going to enter?" Papa repeated.

Erika looked over toward the field. She could see Kari and several others getting ready for the race. Part of Erika wanted to just watch the race, standing safely beside her parents. But part of her wanted to enter the race and show the others that she was eager to participate and make friends—eager to become "one of them."

"Yes," she said. "I do—will—drive in race. With Silky."

"Good!" Mr. Lindstrom said. "But watch out for Kari and Max. They've won every year for three years."

Erika hurried to get Silky and the wagon ready. After she bridled and hitched Silky, Erika guided the horse and wagon into place. She ended up beside

Kari and Max. Erika smiled over at Kari. Kari did smile back, but then she looked calmly at Erika and said, "You won't win. I always win, every year. I use the prize money to have a party for my friends."

Erika hadn't understood all of it. She heard the words "win" and "party," and she'd seen Kari smile for the first time. *Maybe everything will be fine and we'll be friends,* Erika thought happily.

Erika watched a crowd gather in the distance at the finish line. Two poles with red flags staked in the ground marked the end of the race. A team of men loaded four heavy barrels into the back of each wagon. The winning horse would have to be fast and strong to win.

Erika focused her attention on Silky. The powerful horse stamped one front foot and then a hind foot. She shook her head. *She's eager to go,* Erika thought. The horses, lined up in a row, whinnied back and forth to each other, feeling the growing tension in the air.

"You can do it, Silky," Erika said in a soft voice. *"I have never known a horse as strong as you."*

A moment later, Mr. Andersson lowered his arm and shouted out an English word that Erika had no trouble understanding: "Go!"

Erika slapped the reins over Silky's back and hollered, "Hup!" Silky shot forward, straining for a moment against the weight of the wagon. Despite the load, Silky moved swiftly with a long, free stride. Still, they trailed Kari and Max from the very start. "Go, Silky, go!" Erika shouted, realizing she had called out in English without thinking about it.

From the corner of her eye, Erika saw one wagon veer suddenly off the course. Four wagons remained in the race. Kari drove Max with all her might. They were at least three wagon lengths ahead of Erika and Silky.

"Go, go, go," Erika urged, keeping one eye on Silky and one on the finish line. Little by little they gained speed until they were exactly even with Kari. The barrels bumped and thudded in the back of the wagon as Silky's hooves pounded the dirt. The sound was inescapable, and Erika's heart pounded along with it.

Then Silky pulled ahead of Max, first a wagon length and then two. Erika couldn't believe it! But she stayed focused on the course and on guiding Silky over the rough ground.

"Good girl!" Erika exclaimed. "Faster, faster! Go!" She didn't dare look back to see where Kari's wagon was.

But then Silky's front hoof hit a deep rut, and she stumbled. She righted herself quickly, but in doing so veered sharply to the side. Keeping her wits about her, Erika gave a firm tug on the reins and brought Silky immediately back on course.

Kari had regained her lead. She looked back at Erika, her eyes flaming. Erika concentrated on Silky. *"You deserve to win,"* she told the horse.

The end of the race was in sight, with the red flags clearly visible. Erika gave one final "Hup!" and sat forward on the seat. "Go, go, go!" she chanted. Silky lunged forward with a renewed effort, and in four strides they passed the red flags and the blur of the cheering crowd. A moment later Max and Kari crossed the finish. Silky had won the race!

Once she'd slowed the wagon to a stop, Erika was surrounded by people. "You won!" they shouted. "Congratulations!" Her parents ran to her, beaming with pride, and Lise jumped up and down, screaming with joy. Erika was surprised and overjoyed. How wonderful it felt to win and to have so many people smiling at her and congratulating her.

"You showed good thinking," her father told her as he helped her down. "When Silky stumbled, you acted fast."

"It was Silky who did it, Papa. I can't take all the credit. She's strong and she obeys commands."

"You are strong, too," Mama added. *"Stronger than you know."*

Erika looked around for Kari. She wanted to congratulate her on the exciting race. She thought how wonderful it would be for the two of them to go off together and talk about the close finish. They would have something in common now. She walked right up to Kari, not worrying about her English. Kari, too, was surrounded by friends and family. Erika touched her shoulder and said, "Thank you for the—I thank you for the good time." Immediately she thought, *No, that's not right. That's not what I meant.* "I mean, I am happy for you—"

"You mean you're happy for yourself," Kari snapped. "You and your brute of a horse. Why didn't you just stay in Germany where you belong!"

Erika was stunned. She didn't have to know English well to know that Kari was angry, lashing out at her with furious eyes and a taunting voice. Tears welled up in Erika's eyes. How could she have been so wrong? How could she have thought that entering the race with Kari would bring them closer? She was wrong about everything! The language, the people, the customs, everything!

Erika turned and walked slowly away, tears now falling freely down her face. Where could she go? Where could she hide? *This is the worst day of my life!* she thought.

Mrs. Lindstrom came up behind her, trying to soothe Erika and apologize for her daughter. Erika shrugged out of her embrace and ran toward her wagon.

Mr. Andersson stood by Silky, pinning a blue ribbon to her harness. "I have a certificate for you, Erika," he said. "It's worth three dollars of goods at my store. Congratulations!"

But Erika didn't hear his words. Her face was buried in the thick softness of Silky's neck.

CHAPTER THREE

School Daze

"F*inish your breakfast, Erika,"* Mama said. *"Your oatmeal will get cold."*

But Erika had no appetite. The very thought of food made her feel sick. In fact, she hoped she was getting sick. Then she could go back to bed and pull up the covers and forget all about starting school.

She stared up at the high shelf that held Mama's fragile possessions—a glass vase, some painted china plates, and her beloved glass snowball that Papa had given her long ago. Looking at the beautiful objects reminded Erika of her homeland.

"Do you think I have a fever, Mama?" Erika asked. She put a hopeful hand to her forehead. Mama

hurried over and felt Erika's head and cheeks with the back of her hand.

"You feel fine, Erika. What's troubling you?"

"I don't want to go to school," Erika confessed. *"Please don't make me go!"*

Lise finished her bread with jam and took a long drink of milk. *"You're lucky!"* she said. *"I wish I was old enough to go to school and play with all the other children. I have to stay home with Mama."*

Erika envied her little sister. She got to stay home in their cozy house, playing with her doll or helping Mama with chores or running outside to play in the garden and see how big the pumpkins were growing. She didn't have to face a room full of strangers she couldn't talk to.

"You have a case of nerves, Erika," Mama explained. *"After a few days, you'll feel at home."*

No, I won't, Erika thought. *I'll never feel at home here.*

Just then Papa came in from the barn with two full milk pails balanced in his hands. "Silky is hitched," he announced. "She's ready for—to take you to the school. Are you ready, also? School?" he repeated.

"Yes, Papa," answered Erika. She realized that complaining about school to Papa would do no good at all. He was very serious about wanting his daughters to go to school. He thought reading, writing, and arithmetic were as important as farming and building.

Reluctantly, Erika tied her kerchief under her chin, buttoned her sweater, and pulled on her boots. Mama handed her a covered tin pail that held her noon dinner.

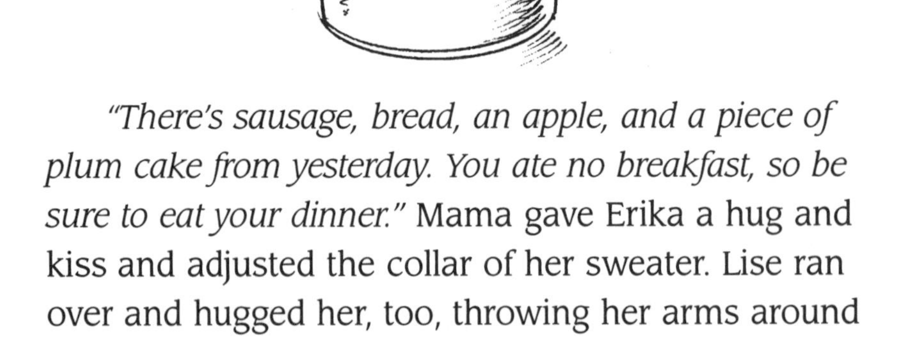

"There's sausage, bread, an apple, and a piece of plum cake from yesterday. You ate no breakfast, so be sure to eat your dinner." Mama gave Erika a hug and kiss and adjusted the collar of her sweater. Lise ran over and hugged her, too, throwing her arms around Erika's waist and holding on tightly.

The trip to Silver Lake passed quickly. Erika sat up front next to Papa, holding her dinner pail in her lap. The sun shone strongly, but the air was cold. Silky's breath came out in steamy puffs as she pulled the wagon.

Erika thought about yesterday's race and Silky's triumphant finish. She had to admit that she was impressed. Silky was clearly more than just a patient, hardworking horse. But she could never take the place of Starlight.

They passed the church and shops and finally pulled up to the school. "Here we are, yes?" Papa said, patting Erika's shoulder. Erika sat frozen in her seat. She couldn't make her legs move to get out of the wagon. Groups of children ran and laughed in the school yard, enjoying the brisk, autumn morning.

"I have to go, Erika," Papa said. "I'm helping Mr. Olsen build his stable. I'll be back for you, after. Be smart. And speak in English, please."

"Yes, Papa," Erika managed to say. She gave him a weak smile and jumped down.

Just then, Silky nickered and threw her head back. Erika walked over and patted her warm brown neck. Silky nickered again and tossed her head in the direction of the school.

"I go! Don't worry!" Erika said, laughing in spite of herself.

Erika waved to Papa and Silky and turned to face the school. Right in front of her stood Kari and another girl, staring at her with hard, cold eyes.

Oh, no! thought Erika. *Now what?* She decided to

be strong and forced a bright, "Hello."

"Look, Birgit," Kari said. "It's the new girl. She may have won the wagon race, but she's not that bright. See, she can't say anything at all. She just stands there."

Birgit shook her curly blonde hair and laughed with Kari. Though Erika missed many of the words, there was no mistaking the message. Erika wished with all her heart that she had never entered the wagon contest. The thrill of winning had quickly disappeared in the dark cloud of Kari's resentment.

Erika quickly brushed past the girls and climbed the steps to the open door. Inside, narrow wooden tables and chairs lined the room, with an aisle in the middle.

It doesn't look much different from my old school in Germany, Erika thought.

In the front of the room, the teacher, a pretty young woman, sat at a large desk, writing. She wore her red-brown hair swept up in a soft bun, and she had wire-rimmed eyeglasses.

Erika approached her and cleared her throat. The woman looked up and smiled. "Good morning," Erika said carefully. "My name is Erika Meyer. I is—am—new girl. Age eleven, please."

"Good morning, Erika Meyer!" the teacher replied.

"I'm pleased to meet you. My name is Miss McGrath."

"Miss McGrath," Erika repeated. "Thank you."

"Welcome to our school, Erika. Let me see," she continued, looking at a list on her desk. "You are from Germany, and you're in the fifth class. Let me show you around."

Miss McGrath showed Erika where to hang her sweater and the shelf for storing dinner pails. Then she directed her to a seat. Erika sat down, relieved that her teacher was friendly and cheerful. She still couldn't forget the sting of Kari's words and the look in her eyes. *If only someone nice would sit next to me,* Erika thought, *I could make it through today.*

Miss McGrath rang the bell on her desk, and soon all the children piled into the room, pink-cheeked and out of breath from playing.

Miss McGrath rapped on her desk for attention, and the room grew silent.

She assigned each student to a seat, and to Erika's horror, Kari was to sit to her left and Birgit to her right. "That way," explained the teacher, "you'll have helpers on either side. They both speak excellent English."

Kari and Birgit reluctantly sat down, but they didn't dare tease Erika in front of the teacher. Erika stared at her hands, praying for the day to pass quickly.

Miss McGrath moved swiftly to the lessons, beginning with arithmetic. Each child, from youngest to oldest, came forward and tried to solve a problem on the blackboard.

I can do this, Erika thought. *It's just numbers, not words.* And sure enough, she easily found the answer to her multiplication problem.

"Excellent," beamed Miss McGrath. "Your turn, Kari."

Erika was surprised at how hard Kari struggled over a simple problem. She got it wrong twice, and then the teacher showed her how to solve it. Erika couldn't help thinking that if she and Kari were friends, she could help her with numbers, and Kari could help her with words.

After arithmetic, Miss McGrath announced it was time for spelling. Just as before, each student came forward to write a word on the blackboard.

Erika's heart pounded as she approached the front of the class again. *I can't spell in English!* she thought.

Miss McGrath smiled and touched Erika's shoulder. "I know you're just learning, Erika. But why not try a word. Let's see—how about *good*? I'll use it in a sentence. 'Erika is a *good* student.' Now you try. *Good.*"

Erika stood there, unable to spell the simple word. In German she could spell much more difficult words. Long words! This was so frustrating! Finally, she scribbled a few letters on the board.

After Miss McGrath had corrected her spelling, Erika shuffled past Kari, head down, and slumped in her seat. Kari rolled her eyes in disgust and passed a note to Birgit. Birgit opened the note and snickered quietly. But not quietly enough.

"Birgit!" Miss McGrath called out. "Come to the front of the class and share your note with all of us."

Birgit looked pleadingly at the teacher and then at Kari.

"Now!" Miss McGrath ordered.

Birgit unfolded the note and cleared her throat. She took a deep breath and read in a barely audible voice, "She's as stupid as her horse."

The class was absolutely still. A fly buzzed by the window. Miss McGrath's nose and cheeks flushed red with anger. "You have behaved with disrespect. I'm deeply ashamed of both you and Kari. Leave the classroom this minute and sit on the steps until dinner. Please think about what it felt like when *you* were new to this place."

Erika understood that Kari and Birgit were in trouble because of the note and that the note had been about her. Instead of feeling happy or relieved that Miss McGrath was punishing them, Erika felt awful. She knew that this event would only make them hate her more. If only Miss McGrath hadn't seen the note, she might still have had a chance to fit in.

When dinner break finally arrived, Erika sat in her seat until everyone claimed their pails and went outside.

Miss McGrath came to her and sat down. "I'm sorry, Erika, for what happened. I won't tolerate unkindness in my students. Now, go enjoy your dinner. It will get better each day, I promise."

Miss McGrath busied herself at her desk. Erika took her pail and left, wishing she could stay inside and eat at her table. Instead, she sat by herself under a willow tree. Not far from her sat Kari, Birgit, and several others, laughing and talking and sharing food.

Erika opened her pail and something flew out in her face! Whoosh! And then another and another! Erika screamed with surprise and jumped up, knocking over her dinner.

Everyone turned to look at her, and then Kari announced, "Look! She brings grasshoppers for her dinner!" This caused a riot of laughter across the school yard.

Erika looked at her upset dinner and then at Kari

and Birgit. *They must have put the grasshoppers in my pail when they came in from being sent outside,* she realized. *They must have been waiting for me to open my pail so they could have a good laugh.*

Tears threatened to spill from her eyes, but Erika would not let them fall. She refused to cry in front of her tormentors. She forced herself to take a bite of her bread and then another. She could barely swallow because of the lump in her throat. Trying to be calm, she ate her apple and her cake.

How will I get through the afternoon? Erika thought. *How long until Papa and Silky come to get me?* Thinking of Papa gave her the incentive she needed to go back into the school. He wanted so much for her to succeed in school. He worked so hard for his dream of a better future for his family.

And strangely, thinking of Silky gave Erika some comfort, too. She wasn't Starlight and never could be. But by now, she was one of the most familiar things in Erika's life. Erika knew her smell, how her coat felt, how hard she worked, her nickers of pleasure and snorts of impatience.

Without fail, Silky always made it clear that she was happy to see Erika. The mare's affection was steady and dependable. And right now, that meant everything.

Moving Again

"*It's a good thing you have such a thick, warm coat,"* Erika told Silky as she groomed her with a stiff brush. *"It's cold here in America, and it's only the end of October.* Erika shivered in the drafty barn, wishing she'd worn gloves to do her chores.

Silky stood patiently, her ears pricked forward, enjoying Erika's brush strokes.

"I wish I could be patient like you, Silky," Erika said. *"I'm so impatient all the time. I feel as if I won't ever have friends or feel at home here or learn to speak English properly."*

Erika finished her brushing and made sure Silky had fresh water and feed in her buckets. Then she took some dried apple from her pocket and held it in her open palm. Silky snorted and munched her treat. Lately, Erika always made sure she saved a bit of fruit or vegetable to give to Silky.

Back inside, Erika sat by the fire to warm herself. She liked Saturdays because when her chores were done, she had a little extra time to herself. Mama and Lise were picking the last of the apples and Papa was working, so she had the house to herself. And she didn't have to go to school, which was the best thing about Saturdays.

She liked Miss McGrath very much, but after the first awful days of class, Kari and her friends chose to ignore Erika with an icy coldness that hurt as much as their teasing and taunting. Most days, Erika ate her dinner and played with the younger students. But even though the little girls were sweet to her, Erika's isolation from friends her age was painful and embarrassing.

Papa interrupted Erika's thoughts about school when he sat next to her on the bench by the fire. He smelled of newly split logs, which he had been chopping all morning. "It is time to—now is time for me to talk, Erika."

Erika's heart skipped a beat. *He sounds so serious,* she thought. *Like when he told us we were moving to*

America. Erika wondered what terrible thing was about to happen. "Yes?" she said, her eyes wide with worry.

"Don't frown so!" Papa laughed. "I have good news."

Then he began speaking so fast and excitedly in English that Erika had to say, "Whoa!" just the way she did to slow Silky and the wagon.

Papa broke his rule and spoke in German so Erika would understand everything. *"We're moving to town, Erika. To Silver Lake. Just for the winter."*

"We are?" Erika exclaimed. *"Why?"*

Papa reached over and loosened his boot lace. *"Everyone is predicting a terrible winter this year. Mama and I are worried that this house won't be warm enough."*

"But where will we live?"

"Per Andersson's daughter and son-in-law have moved to the Dakota Territory and their house is vacant. It has a barn for Silky, and the rent is reasonable."

"What will you do in town, Papa? For work, I mean?"

"Carpentry. Silver Lake is growing fast, and there will be so much new construction."

Erika was silent for a moment, taking in Papa's news. The last thing she wanted was to move again.

It had taken so long to get settled on the farm, and now they had to move yet again. Before coming to America, Erika had lived in the same place her entire life. Now nothing stayed the same.

"And do you want to know the best thing of all?" Papa asked.

"What?" Erika whispered, not sure she wanted to know.

"Our new house is close to school, so you'll never have to miss a day, even in bad weather."

Erika clapped a hand over her mouth so she wouldn't say anything that might hurt Papa's feelings. She hadn't told him how difficult things were at school. Papa so wanted for her to love America and love her school. She didn't have the heart to burden him with the truth.

"Con-grat-u-lations, Papa," she finally said, in slow, careful English. "It will be—happy."

"You mean *we* will be happy," Papa said. "Very good with the English," he added, giving her a hug. "Ach, I nearly forgot! I have an important job for you once we move to Silver Lake."

"What, Papa? Take care of Silky? I already do that."

"Per Andersson's son-in-law used to meet the morning train and bring the mail bag to Andersson's store. Now that he's gone, Per Andersson needs

someone to take his place and bring the mail."

"You mean me, Papa?"

"Yes. Each morning, you'll take Silky and the wagon and drive over to meet the train. It will mean being a few minutes late to school, but the money from Per Andersson will help our family. What do you think?"

Erika was honored to be asked to help. It made her proud to know that she could contribute to her family. Papa and Mama worked so hard in America, the least she could do was drive the wagon once a day. But would it matter to Miss McGrath if she came late to school? She'd have to talk with her soon.

"I will," Erika told Papa. *"I will be the mail girl of Silver Lake!"*

Papa hugged her again, and then Lise came bursting through the door with Mama close behind her.

"We're moving to Silver Lake!" Lise shouted. *"Did you hear, Erika? We're moving to Silver Lake! Mama says I can skate on the pond and go to church, and we can maybe buy candy sometimes at the store and–"*

"I heard, I heard!" Erika laughed, grabbing her sister and pulling her into her lap. *"I'm glad you're so excited."*

"Aren't you?" Lise asked, twisting away. *"Aren't you?"*

Erika nodded and tried to smile at her sister. Every change was exciting to Lise, and Mama and Papa were cheerful, no matter what. *I've had enough change,* Erika thought. But she tried to smile anyway.

"I'll need your help this afternoon," Mama said. *"We need to pack so Papa can start taking wagon loads to the new house. It's all happening so quickly."*

Erika stood and stretched. So much for her Saturday leisure time. She might as well accept the new move and get busy. *"Yes, Mama,"* she said. *"Where shall we begin?"*

"Let's see," Mama said, looking around the house. *"I'll start with the kitchen. Lise, you pack the linens and clothing. Erika, why don't you pack whatever is fragile on the shelf."*

Erika brought out the rag bag so she could pack the half dozen fragile items in clean cloths and nestle them in a straw-filled barrel. She carefully wrapped a painted china plate and then a vase made of deep blue glass.

Touching the familiar objects that came from their old life in Germany made Erika deeply sad. Each item held special memories—a certain Christmas spent with cousins, the birth of Lise, mementos from grandparents, a framed photograph of her parents' wedding day.

At least, thought Erika, *we will always have these same special things, no matter where we move.*

She reached for the last and most prized possession of all—the snowball. The delicate glass orb had been Papa's engagement present to Mama, made by the best craftsman in their town.

Erika shook it lightly. Flecks of paper snow whirled around the miniature town inside the glass. The tiny houses, shops, and people were carved from wood and looked so realistic that Erika was instantly transported back to Germany.

For as long as she could remember, the snowball had been part of her life. Mama always dusted it carefully and placed it on the highest shelf in the house. Erika hadn't even been allowed to hold it until she turned ten. All the way to America, on the big steamer ship, Mama had worried about the snowball, stored in a packing crate below the decks.

Lise danced over to Erika with her doll in her hand. *"The snowball! Shake it for me, Erika! Let me see it snow!"*

Carefully, Erika shook the snowball and held it out in both of her hands for Lise to see.

Lise stared at the flying snow, mesmerized by the scene. *"I love it, I love it!* she chanted, spinning in a circle like the snow.

"Be careful!" Mama warned, turning from the stove. *"Slow down, Lise!"*

"Stop!" Erika cried.

But Lise kept spinning, her doll in her hand. Erika tried to move out of the way, but it was too late. Lise crashed into her sister, pushing Erika right into the wall. The snowball flew from Erika's hands and broke against the hard wooden floor.

The sound of the glass splintering was the most awful thing Erika had ever heard.

For a shocked moment, no one said a word. Even Lise was silent. Erika, frozen in place, looked with horror at Mama. Wordlessly, Mama crossed the room and knelt down on the floor.

Lise began to cry, saying over and over, *"I'm sorry, Mama. I'm sorry, Mama. I didn't mean to. I didn't mean to."*

Erika watched as her mother picked up the wooden carving of the town and the snowball's wooden pedestal. Both were unharmed. Mama placed them in the barrel with the other things and sank down in her rocking chair. She put her face in her hands and cried softly. Lise ran to Mama and climbed into her lap. Mama and Lise rocked together, both of them crying.

Erika didn't know what to do. Mama so rarely cried, and when she did it was usually what she called "happy tears." She cried when she heard children singing or when she heard the news that a healthy baby had been born. She cried on Christmas Eve when she lit the candles on the tree. But she never cried sad tears. She hadn't cried when they left Germany or on the long journey to America.

Erika got the broom and swept the broken glass into the dustbin. *Mama must be homesick, too,* Erika realized. *Even though she's strong and never says a harsh word, this is hard for her, too. I'm not the only one.*

After a time, Mama blew her nose and took a deep breath. *"Well,"* she said, *"I think I've cried all my tears for the next hundred years."*

"Me, too," sniffed Lise. *"Two hundred years. Three hundred years!"*

"I'm sorry, Mama," Erika said. *"Is there anything I can do?"*

"No, Erika," Mama said. *"Accidents happen. Now I need to stir the soup and bake the bread for dinner."*

Gently, Mama eased Lise off her lap and went to stir the fragrant cabbage soup. *"Let's go outside,"* Erika whispered to Lise. *"Give Mama some peace."*

Lise nodded and took Erika's hand. They went out to the barn to visit Silky, who was dozing in her stall. While Lise patted and nuzzled the horse, Erika tried to think of a plan.

I have to find a way to fix the snowball, she thought. Christmas was only two months away, and Erika thought how wonderful it would be to give the repaired snowball to Mama for a Christmas gift.

Erika joined Lise next to Silky and stroked the mare's neck.

"She's a pretty horse," Lise said. *"I like the white on her brown face, don't you? And she won the race, remember? Remember when you and Silky won the wagon race?"*

Erika nodded at Lise, wishing she could be as carefree as her sister. *"Silky's a good horse,"* Erika said, smoothing the mare's brown mane. *"She's a good, strong horse."*

Silky stamped her feet and shook her head,

looking right at Erika. Erika had the strange feeling that Silky knew something she didn't—knew part of the story she couldn't even guess at yet.

"What?" Erika said in English. "What is it that you know?"

Silky continued to stare at Erika with her big brown eyes that seemed to say, "Just wait. Be patient and wait."

CHAPTER FIVE

Winter Dark

"Always it is dark!" Erika whispered, peering out the window of her small bedroom.

December was a dark month in Silver Lake. It was pitch black when Erika arose in the mornings and dark when she walked home from school in the afternoons. Even when the sun shone, it was a thin, weak daylight with layers of gray clouds. The only good thing about December, as far as she was concerned, was that Christmas would be coming soon.

Erika hurried out of her flannel nightclothes, hopping back and forth to keep warm. She scrambled into her wool leggings and undershirt, flannel dress, wool sweater, wool socks, and knitted scarf. She envied Lise who slept cozily under the quilts of the bed they shared, lucky enough to have several more hours of sleep ahead of her.

In the kitchen, Mama and Papa drank steaming coffee by the stove, already dressed and ready for their day to begin. Erika ate her oatmeal and bread and drank a cup of blackberry tea. In the mornings, they each went about their tasks quietly, trying to wake up and get warm.

Their daily routine began with early mornings for all of them. Papa tended to Silky and hitched her to the wagon. Then, after Erika ate breakfast and bundled up, she left for her short drive to the train station and general store. Mama had cooking and home chores to tend to, and Papa set out for his various building jobs. Then Erika drove Silky home and hurried off to school on foot. In the evenings, there were more chores, homework, and the dark, cold nights. Erika couldn't remember a busier time for her family!

"Good-bye," Erika called to her parents. Mama kissed her and gave her two steaming potatoes from the stove. Erika slipped them into her coat pockets. Later she would use them to warm her hands.

"Be sure to wrap yourself in the blankets," Mama reminded her.

Erika braced herself for the blast of cold air outside the door. Silky stamped her feet in the snow, eager as always to get going.

"Good morning, Silky," Erika said, stroking the mare's neck. Silky nickered and nodded her head.

"Hup!" Erika called, from the front of the wagon, and the horse took off, her feet making a crunching sound in the snow.

Even with the early hour and biting cold, Erika looked forward to her morning rides with Silky. The world was still and beautiful at that time of day. To make herself forget about the cold, Erika had taken to singing her favorite songs in German as they made their way to the station. Erika's voice rang loud and clear and beautiful in the frozen air.

Lately, she had added Christmas carols to her repertoire, and she secretly believed that Silky approved. Silky seemed to high step through the snow with her showy stride, in rhythm with Erika's singing. During those moments, Erika felt peaceful. She didn't think about being lonely, nor worry about her English, nor wonder if Kari would ever get over her anger.

That morning Erika concentrated especially hard on her singing. For in school that very day, Miss McGrath was holding auditions for the upcoming Christmas pageant. Any student who wished to recite or sing a solo at the annual Christmas festival had to perform in front of Miss McGrath. Erika loved Christmas and thought how proud Mama and Papa would be to hear her sing at a town festival. Christmas celebrations had been an important part of their life in Germany.

"Stille Nacht, heilige Nacht," Erika sang, *"alles schläft, einsam wacht . . ."* It was Erika's favorite carol. The music was written in 1818 by an Austrian composer named Franz Gruber.

Erika found the melody and lyrics so moving that the carol sometimes brought tears to her eyes when she heard it. *Happy tears, just like Mama,* Erika thought. She knew the carol was popular in America, too, though she didn't know any words beyond, "Silent night, holy night . . ."

After picking up the mail from the morning train, Erika drove Silky back to Per Andersson's store. She hitched Silky outside and gave her some carrots and dried apple to snack on while she went into the store.

"Good morning!" Erika called to Mr. and Mrs. Andersson.

"Good morning, Miss Mail Lady," they always joked.

Erika loved to visit with the Anderssons. They were friendly and generous, always offering her a pastry or a cup of hot cocoa before she left for school.

"Don't forget," Mr. Andersson said as he opened the bag of mail, "you haven't spent your three-dollar credit in the store."

Erika was pleased to have understood his words. "Yes. This is true," she agreed. "I think—perhaps—for Christmas."

"A special gift?" Mrs. Andersson asked, handing Erika a cup of cocoa.

"Yes. Gift. For my mama and papa. And Lise, too."

"How nice you are," said Mr. Andersson. "You'll have to look around and decide soon."

Erika tried to explain that she needed to hurry to school for the auditions and couldn't linger. She didn't want to miss her chance to sing. She stumbled on her words and finally stammered, "To not be late—and I must go."

After returning Silky and the wagon, Erika ran all the way to school, singing under her breath. When she finally opened the creaky door, her classmates were busily working at their seats.

"Good morning, Erika," Miss McGrath said.

"Good morning," Erika said, cautiously approaching Miss McGrath's desk. "Excuse me," she said. "Are I—I mean—am I late for singing?"

"I'm afraid you are," Miss McGrath said. "I know

you have an extra chore in the morning, but I thought it wouldn't be fair to make everyone wait and get more nervous."

Erika understood enough. She had missed her chance. Her only chance to sing at the Christmas festival. She turned to go to her seat and saw Kari staring at her with a satisfied expression. *I can't seem to do anything right, here,* Erika thought. The contentment she had felt earlier when she was singing to Silky evaporated completely.

"Wait a moment, Erika," Miss McGrath said.

Erika turned around. "Yes?" she said, trying to sound composed.

"I didn't say you couldn't audition, dear. I only meant that everyone else has already finished. Please go ahead."

"What?" asked Erika, not certain she had understood.

"Sing, Erika! Sing your song!"

"Now?" Erika asked, looking at the more than twenty students staring at her curiously.

"Yes," Miss McGrath repeated. "Go ahead."

Erika cleared her throat and straightened her sagging shoulders. Her cheeks flushed with embarrassment at the sudden attention focused on her audition. *I hope my voice doesn't crack,* she thought.

She pretended that she was back in the wagon, singing to Silky as they spun along the road. She thought of Silky's strong, high gait keeping time with her song. She took a deep breath and began.

"Stille Nacht, heilige Nacht,
alles schläft, einsam wacht
nur das traute, hochheilige Paar. . ."

It was working. As Erika imagined singing to Silky she forgot her nervousness. She concentrated on the simple beauty of the song and the many memories of her home in Germany that it brought back to her. When she finished, the room was silent. For a moment Erika thought she had done something wrong. Even Miss McGrath sat quietly at her desk.

Then Miss McGrath stood and softly applauded Erika's singing. The children joined in, too, with the exception of Kari and Birgit.

Erika was stunned by the clapping. It jarred her back to reality. She blushed again and looked at Miss McGrath and shrugged with confusion.

"That was beautiful, Erika. You have a lovely voice, and I enjoyed hearing the song in its original language."

"Thank you," Erika managed to say. She realized she was being complimented, and it made her tingle with happiness.

"Of course you will sing a solo at the Christmas festival. In fact, you must sing that very song. But I'd like it if you'd sing it in both German and English. Would that be all right?"

Erika shook her head. She wasn't following Miss McGrath very well.

Miss McGrath spoke slowly, "For the Christmas festival, sing in English, too."

"Yes," Erika agreed, now understanding Miss McGrath's instructions. She would get to sing "Stille Nacht" at the festival, but she had to learn the English words. *Perhaps Per Andersson will help me,* Erika thought as she took her seat next to Kari.

For the rest of the day, Erika beamed. She couldn't wait to tell Papa and Mama and Lise. Lise would be so excited. Erika could see her jumping and spinning when she heard the news. And wait until she told Silky! She would have to practice every morning on their way to the station.

The only dark cloud over her wonderful day was Kari Lindstrom. All through lessons she "accidentally" stepped on the hem of Erika's dress with her boot, pressing down harder each time Erika tried to ease the fabric away. It was nothing that anyone else would even notice. If she told Miss McGrath, Kari would innocently proclaim that it had been an accident and that she was extremely sorry.

Why must she spoil everything? Erika thought. *What did I ever do to her besides beat her in a silly wagon race? And why does Birgit always follow Kari's lead?*

Erika worked these thoughts over in her head all afternoon, until Miss McGrath finally rang the bell for dismissal. All the children scattered from their seats and dashed to get their coats and supper pails. Erika sat alone, waiting until she was the last one left in the schoolroom.

Miss McGrath looked up from her desk and noticed Erika. "Yes? What can I do for you?" she asked kindly.

Erika stood politely and carefully formed her words. "Please, if you can to—if you will—I need for the . . ."

"Take your time, Erika," Miss McGrath said. "I'm listening. I know it's hard."

"Please the words to song in the English," she finally stated.

"Ah, of course! You would like me to write out the English words to the song so you can learn them. Correct?"

"Yes!" smiled Erika, pleased to have made her point.

"I'll do it right now," said Miss McGrath. "And

while I do that, would you help me by erasing the blackboard?"

She handed Erika the eraser, and Erika immediately understood. As she erased the words on the board, she wished she could as easily erase the many mistakes she felt she had made—mistakes with language, mistakes trying to make friends, the mistake of the broken snowball at home, the mistake of not treating Silky as well as she had once treated Starlight.

"Are you finished?" Miss McGrath asked.

Erika put down the eraser and faced her teacher.

Miss McGrath handed her a paper printed with words in English. "There you are," she said. "Let me know if you need any help with the words."

"Thank you," Erika said, giving a formal curtsey. She moved to get her coat, but Miss McGrath called her back.

"I was wondering, Erika," she said, taking off her spectacles and rubbing her nose, "how you learned to sing so well. Do you practice?"

Erika thought for a moment. How could she explain that she practiced by singing each morning to her horse? And that she could tell by Silky's stride if her singing was good! Miss McGrath would never believe her.

Instead, Erika simply answered, "My friend. I sing to my friend."

And it was true. Silky had become Erika's good friend.

CHAPTER SIX

Glass and Ice

"Have you decided on your gifts?" Mr. Andersson asked Erika. It was Saturday morning, two weeks before Christmas, and Erika was choosing presents for her family from the general store.

"I am looking, still," Erika said. "There is so many—I mean much—to see."

"Take your time," Mr. Andersson said. "You're my first customer this morning."

Erika wandered around the store, studying the barrels and bins filled with holiday goods. There was so much to choose from! Oranges and

English walnuts and candy of every kind. Bolts of fabric and spools of ribbon. Glass beads and writing paper and candles and toys!

She finally decided on a green hair ribbon and some butterscotch candies for Lise. She discovered a pair of handsome brass buttons for Papa's suspenders, to replace the cracked wooden ones he currently had.

She even found a bag of "horse candy" for Silky, which was really an assortment of dried fruit and special grain.

"I'll take these," Erika told Mr. Andersson, putting her items on the counter.

"What about for Mama?" he asked. "You didn't see anything you liked?"

Erika shook her head sadly. What she wanted for Mama couldn't be bought at any store. She told Mr. Andersson about the shattered snowball and how she wanted to replace it in time for Christmas.

"I know just the person to help you," Mr. Andersson said slowly. "Have you heard of Gunnar Dahlberg?"

Erika shook her head.

"People call him the Glass Man. He lives alone in the woods. He's very old now, and I'm not sure if he still makes much glass."

Erika's heart leapt. "How could I find him?"

"I will draw you a map. But, Erika, I can't make any promises that he'll help you."

"I will go anyway," Erika stated firmly. "I must try."

Mr. Andersson added up Erika's purchases. "That comes to eighty-five cents. With your three-dollar credit, I owe you two dollars and fifteen cents." He counted out the change and wrapped the presents with brown paper and string. Then he drew a map to the Glass Man's cottage.

"Thank you!" Erika exclaimed. "Thank you for everything. You are the most—of all people—the nicest one!"

Erika hurried home and asked Mama to let her take Silky and the wagon.

"It's important, Mama. And it's a secret—for Christmas. Please say yes!"

Mama looked doubtful, but she agreed. *"Be careful, Erika,"* she said. *"The road is icy. Don't go too fast."*

"Can I go, too?" Lise asked. *"Please!"*

"I thought you wanted to go ice skating with your friend Oskar?" Mama said.

"I forgot, I forgot!" Lise said happily. *"I'd rather go ice skating than ride in the wagon."*

Erika found the wooden pedestal and carved scenery from the broken snowball and hid them under her coat. Then she slipped out of the house and ran to the barn to hitch up Silky.

"Hello, girl," she called to her horse. "We have a—how do you say it?—an adventure!" Silky raised her thick brown tail and snorted.

Erika remembered when she didn't believe that she and Silky would ever have adventures together. And yet, here they were, off to meet an old glassmaker who lived in a cottage in the woods!

All the way there, over icy roads, Erika practiced her Christmas carol for Silky. Silky responded with her high steps and easy stride, pulling the wagon along as though it were as light as the breeze.

"Silent night, holy night," Erika sang, "all is calm, all is bright. . ." *At least I know the beginning,* she thought. *And I have a week and a half to practice the rest.*

After they crossed Beaver Creek, Erika pulled the wagon over to the side of the road. She studied the map and then looked up to find the last landmark.

"There it is, Silky! See that clump of tall pine trees? We're almost there."

A few minutes later she spotted a cottage with a thin curl of smoke coming from the chimney.

Erika brought Silky to a halt outside the cottage and reached under the seat for the broken snowball wrapped in cloth. She slowly approached the door, summoning her courage. What if the Glass Man was mean? What if he wasn't home? What if he couldn't help?

She knocked three times on the wooden door and waited. She looked back at Silky who stood proudly and patiently, head up, watching Erika. Then the door opened, and Erika looked into the bright eyes of a short, wrinkled man with a frizz of white hair.

"Yes?" he asked, peering at Erika and her horse and wagon.

"Mr. Dahlberg?"

"Yes," he replied. "Who might you be?"

Erika introduced herself, hugging her parcel tighter to her chest. "I need some glass," she tried to explain. "For my mama, for her—how do you say it—?" Silky snorted, giving Erika encouragement to continue. "Here, I show you."

Erika unwrapped her package and showed the two pieces to Mr. Dahlberg. "Here," she said. "You see?"

Mr. Dahlberg picked up the pedestal and scenery and examined them while Erika stood shivering on the steps.

"I can fix it," he said, looking at Erika. "I can make a new glass globe."

Erika smiled at Mr. Dahlberg, elated at his answer.

"How long? And, please, how much?" she asked.

"Hmmm," he mused, looking off at the pale sky. "Come inside."

Erika stepped into the warmth. The sight before her eyes was truly magnificent. All around, on shelves, tables, and the floor, was glass of all kinds—glass vases, drinking glasses, ornaments, and picture frames. The room sparkled with shiny, delicate glass. Erika instantly was glad that Lise hadn't come with her. *Imagine her dancing around this room!* she thought.

Mr. Dahlberg looked at a calendar on his wall and then looked back at Erika. "December twenty-fourth it will be ready. In the afternoon."

"That is good!" Erika exclaimed. "It is a special Christmas present for Mama."

"The cost will be four dollars."

Erika's heart sank. Four dollars! She only had a bit more than two dollars. Her eyes brimmed with tears, and she turned for the door, almost forgetting her manners.

"Thank you, sir," she said. "But all I have is two dollars and fifteen cents. I am sorry to bother you." *All this way for nothing,* she thought sadly.

"Wait!" Mr. Dahlberg called. "A moment, please. I have an idea. I will fix your snowball for two dollars.

In return, you will do a small job for me."

"What is it?" she asked eagerly.

"You will deliver two gifts to town for me on your way back."

"Yes! I will be glad to!"

"They go to the church. These two vases are for the Christmas festival. I'll wrap them carefully, and you'll deliver them. Are you a careful driver?"

"Oh, yes," Erika said. "My horse, Silky, is the best wagon horse in town. She's strong and fast."

"You come back on December twenty-fourth," he said, handing Erika the wrapped vases.

"I will. And thank you, Mr. Dahlberg." Erika happily handed him her two dollars.

As Silky pulled the wagon away from the cottage, Erika turned around and saw Mr. Dahlberg standing on the steps waving. "He doesn't seem to get cold," Erika told Silky, as she waved back. "He must like the winter."

She had to admit that sometimes the winter in Silver Lake was very beautiful. Like right now, with a light snow sifting down, fine and glittery, just like the snow inside Mama's snowball.

"Silent night, holy night," Erika sang loud and clear, "all is calm, all is bright!" She felt happier than she had in a long while. The day had been a good one. Soon Christmas would come and then a long vacation from school. She wouldn't have to see Kari and Birgit for weeks.

The trip home went quickly. As they neared the church in Silver Lake, Erika looked toward the skating pond. A lone figure in a blue coat pushed along the ice. As the wagon drew closer, Erika realized the skater was her little sister.

"What is she doing there? Erika said to Silky. *"And where is her friend, Oskar? I know Mama wouldn't want Lise to skate alone on the pond!"*

Erika slapped Silky's reins, urging her toward the pond. She called out to Lise, who looked up and waved. Erika stopped the wagon and jumped out.

"What are you doing here alone?" Erika asked.

"Oskar had to go home. I wanted to go around one more time."

"Come, Lise. Mama will be angry at you. It's dangerous to skate alone. I'll give you a ride."

Just then, Erika heard a terrible, sickening sound. And she knew just what it was.

The ice was cracking!

Stifling an impulse to scream, Erika knew she must remain calm and get Lise off the ice. Now!

"Lise," she said, trying to keep her voice from quaking, *"stay right where you are. Don't move."*

"Why?" Lise smiled, thinking her sister was playing a game of statues.

"Don't move, Lise," Erika said again. *"The ice is cracking in the middle. Stand still."*

Lise seemed to understand the seriousness of Erika's tone and froze where she was. *"I'm scared,"* she said in a small voice.

Looking in the wagon, Erika found a loop of strong rope. She quickly tied it to the back of the wagon and threw it out on the ice as far as she could. It landed several feet from Lise.

"Lise, pick up the rope and tie it around your waist. Pull tight!"

Erika could see that Lise was trembling. When the rope was around her sister's waist, Erika jumped into the wagon. Again she heard the awful thundering of ice breaking apart.

"Silky will pull the wagon, Lise," Erika hollered. *"Try to keep your balance and let the wagon pull you. Do you hear me?"*

Lise didn't answer. She was crying audibly now and shaking with cold.

Erika took a deep breath. "Help me, Silky," she pleaded. "Hup!"

The ice cracked and Lise screamed. Silky lurched forward and the wagon moved. Erika guided the reins

gently, turning Silky to the right to avoid a rutted patch of snow. "Hup!"

Erika turned around. Lise was standing, her arms straight out from her sides, trying to keep her balance as Silky pulled her off the ice.

When Lise at last stumbled to the shore, Erika brought Silky to a halt. Then she ran to hug her frightened little sister. Lise clung to her, sobbing and shivering.

Erika grabbed a blanket from the wagon and wrapped it around Lise. Then she pulled her onto her lap in the front seat of the wagon. She rocked and soothed Lise until she stopped crying.

After removing Lise's skates and searching for her shoes along the shore, Erika turned at last to Silky. She stood next to her and put a hand under the horse's soft white chin, stroking gently. Silky nickered and nuzzled Erika's face.

"Two adventures in one day," Erika said. She put her face against Silky's neck and hugged her.

In German she said, *"Silky, you're the best horse in the world. You saved Lise's life. Please forgive me for not wanting you."*

Silky nickered, and her eyes seemed to say, "All is forgiven. We're a team."

The Christmas Festival

"Hurry, please!" Papa called from downstairs. "Now it is time to go!"

Erika finished buttoning her very best dress—dark blue cotton with an ivory lace collar—and checked her hair in the small hand mirror on her bureau. Instead of her usual braids, she wore her wavy hair down past her shoulders and tied with a blue satin ribbon.

"I look pretty!" she exclaimed, with a mixture of pleasure and surprise. Her cheeks were pink with excitement, and her blue eyes shone. "Silent night, holy night, all is calm, all is bright," she sang as she came down the steep stairs.

"I am ready," she announced to Papa, who stood at the door in his coat. He, too, was dressed in his Sunday church clothes, and Erika thought he looked very handsome. "Where is Mama?"

"She went already to the church. With Mrs. Andersson. She is helping with the ladies—for refreshments."

Erika was proud of Mama. Lately, she had been attending the Ladies Quilting Society and helping with church suppers, despite her lack of English. She always seemed happy when she returned from these activities, and Erika knew it was because she was making friends. Papa was sure that Mama was now ready to learn English.

But Mama teased him and said, *"You don't have to speak the same language to make a quilt or cook a supper. You can stitch and stir in any language."*

"And where is Lise?" Erika asked as she gathered her coat, mittens, and muffler. "It is too quiet."

"Outside in the wagon."

Papa offered his arm to Erika, and she took it happily. Tonight was going to be wonderful! Tonight was the Christmas festival and her very own solo. And it was just two days until Christmas! And best of all, school was over and winter break had officially begun!

Outside in the wagon, Lise sat in the driver's seat,

pretending to drive Silky. She shook the reins and hollered, "Hup!" just like Erika did. But Silky wasn't fooled. She stood, patient and elegant, waiting for Erika. After Erika had taken the reins from her sister, she noticed something different about Silky.

"What is that? There—in her mane?" she asked, pointing. Lise giggled and jumped up and down.

"It looks like maybe ribbon," Papa said. "Red ribbon."

"I put it there! I did it!" Lise shouted. *"Today in the barn, Oskar and I braided her hair and put in my ribbon. We put one in her tail, too!"*

"But why?" Erika asked, laughing in spite of herself.

"Because we wanted her to be dressed up for the party, too! That's why!"

Papa laughed and kissed the top of Lise's head. *"You are mischievous, my little one. You had better be good because Christmas is coming."*

"Hup!" Erika called out, giving the reins a gentle slap. Silky took off for the short, fast drive. Though the church wasn't too far, Papa and Mama were worried that Lise might fall asleep if the party went on too late. With the wagon, they could wrap her in blankets and nestle her in the back for the drive home, instead of carrying her as they walked. Lise had caught a bad cold after the incident at the skating pond, and now Mama fussed over her constantly.

Quietly, Erika practiced her song one more time, watching as Silky lifted her muscular legs high. "Silent night, holy night," she sang, trying to pronounce the words clearly and precisely. Papa, who didn't know the English words, hummed along with her.

"Sing it in German so I can sing!" Lise insisted, and so Erika switched to German.

As she did, she realized that it was becoming easier and easier to go back and forth between the two languages and that, sometimes, she even thought in English. The three of them sang four full verses before they arrived at the church.

Papa told Erika he would tend to Silky and the wagon. "Take Lise with you inside to be warm," he said.

Lise hopped down and took off running toward the open doors of the church, which was quickly filling up with townspeople.

Erika stopped by Silky's side and rested her head on the horse's shoulder. She fingered the red ribbon that Lise had braided into her mane and whispered, "Wish me luck, Silky. I sing, always, for you."

Silky nickered and Erika gave her a quick hug before leaving.

The sight inside the church took Erika's breath away. The large room was aglow with dozens and dozens of candles. Pine boughs hung on every pew, tied with bright ribbons. Silver paper stars decorated the windows. At the front of the church's small alter, Erika spotted the two glass vases made by the Glass Man. They were filled with green holly boughs studded with bright red holly berries. The vases reminded Erika that tomorrow she would pick up the repaired snowball from Mr. Dahlberg.

It's a magical Christmas land, Erika thought, looking around. *A twinkling holiday paradise! And our first Christmas in America.* For a brief moment, Erika thought about her hometown in Germany and how the town square would be decorated. She thought about the feast her cousins and aunts and uncles would share. And she thought about Starlight, who she hoped was warm and happy in her cousins' barn.

Erika waved to Mama in the back of the church. Mama was helping to lay out trays of cookies and glasses for punch and cider. She was laughing at something, and Erika thought she looked young and beautiful. Mama, too, wore her best dress, a deep gray flannel with black buttons and a black sash at the waist. She seemed quite at home with the other ladies, and Erika felt a twinge of envy. Grown-up ladies didn't appear to tease and exclude one another the way children so often did. *What is their secret?* Erika wondered.

Just then, Erika felt a hand on her shoulder. It was Miss McGrath, looking much fancier than she did at school. She wore a deep green dress with a black velvet collar, and her hair was pinned with a tortoise shell comb. "You are beautiful this night!" Erika gasped.

"Thank you, dear," her teacher smiled. "And so are you. It's a very special night. Are you ready? For your song?"

Erika nodded slowly. "Yes. I have practice."

"You mean *practiced,*" Miss McGrath said.

"Yes. Practiced. I sing to my horse."

Miss McGrath laughed at this. "You are a singular girl, Erika. And that's a good thing to be," she added. "It means you are not like everyone else."

Erika understood she was being complimented, but it didn't make her happy. She wanted to be like the other girls. She wanted to be accepted and be one of them.

As if to emphasize her feelings, Kari and Birgit brushed by, laughing and talking, completely ignoring Erika.

Miss McGrath noticed and said to Erika, "I know

it's been hard for you with the other girls. All I can tell you is that when Kari Lindstrom first moved here, she had a hard time, too."

If that was true, Erika wondered, *then why wasn't Kari more understanding? If she knew what it felt like to be a foreigner and feel homesick, then why didn't she reach out a hand of friendship?*

"It's time," Miss McGrath said. "Time to go to the front and begin our program."

Erika joined her fellow students at the front of the church. As everyone took their seats, Mr. Andersson played a tune on his fiddle, tapping his foot in time. Erika watched him with great affection. His friendship meant so much to her. He and Mrs. Andersson and Miss McGrath and Silky were her only true friends in America. *Four friends,* thought Erika. *That's not so bad!*

After Mr. Andersson's tune, Miss McGrath welcomed everyone and read the evening's program. First the younger children would sing together, and then the older students. Finally, there would be solos and recitations, followed by a community sing-a-long and delicious treats.

Erika stood patiently, looking out into the audience while the younger students sang. Everyone was dressed in fancy clothes, and the adults beamed at the children with loving smiles. Erika knew that among the audience there were families from Germany, Sweden, Austria, Denmark, Poland, Russia, Ireland, Scotland, and many other places. So many different people from different lands, coming together to sing and celebrate. It made Erika feel warm and hopeful and full of Christmas spirit. Maybe her first Christmas in America wouldn't be so bad, after all.

Soon it was time for the solos and recitations. Kari went first, speaking about how her family celebrated St. Lucia Day, which was a Swedish custom. Every December 13, she dressed as the Lucia Queen, wearing a special dress and crown of green leaves with lighted candles. Then she served special Lucia buns and coffee to her family for breakfast.

Erika was fascinated. She wanted to hear more about this holiday. It sounded so interesting. How she wished she and Kari were friends so she could ask her all about it.

Next, several other students talked about their holiday customs and read poems they'd composed especially for the occasion. And then it was time for Erika's solo.

"Now," Miss McGrath announced, "Erika Meyer will sing a traditional German carol in both German and English. Please join in for the last chorus."

Erika stepped forward and tried to ignore her

sweating palms and racing heart. *I can do it!* she told herself. Softly at first, she began to sing.

"Stille Nacht, heilige Nacht,
alles schläft, einsam wacht
nur das traute, hochheilige Paar . . ."

Then her voice got louder and more confident, and by the time she reached the final verse, her voice was full and rich. She glanced at her family and saw Mama and Papa wipe tears from their eyes. She knew they were happy tears, and she was so proud she thought she might burst.

When she began the English version, Erika happened to look out the side window of the church. There in plain view was Silky, hitched to a post, staring into the lighted window. *My Silky!* Erika thought. *Here is your song.*

"Silent night, holy night,
all is calm, all is bright . . ."

Erika concentrated on the English words, pretending she was singing to Silky on the way to get the mail. She pictured Silky stepping to the music in the still light of a frosty dawn. It worked, and her pronunciation was close to perfect. She saw Miss McGrath smile at her. On the last verse, the entire audience joined in, and their voices filled the room. *The perfect way to end!* Erika thought.

Everyone applauded at the end of the song, and Erika smiled with relief. She had done it! She had accomplished her goal! She couldn't wait to hug her parents and Lise and talk to Mr. and Mrs. Andersson. She couldn't wait to tell Silky how well she had done.

But from the corner of her eye, Erika noticed that Kari was the only one not clapping. She stared at Erika with her usual frown.

"And now," Miss McGrath announced, "we invite you to share some holiday cheer with us. We thank all the ladies who contributed cookies and punch to our festival. I have a special treat for all my students," she continued, holding up a basket of peppermint sticks. "Kari, would you please be the Lucia Queen and distribute these sweets?"

Kari nodded and bowed and took the basket. Immediately, the students crowded around her to grab a peppermint. Erika decided to wait. She didn't feel brave enough to approach Kari right then.

"Wonderful, wonderful!" Mama said, pulling Erika into an embrace. *"I was so proud of you up there!"*

"And in English!" said Papa, beaming at Erika. "My smart daughter."

Lise ran over and hugged her big sister. *"I liked your singing! You were good! Can I have a bite of your peppermint stick?"*

"Go get your sweet," Mama said. *"You deserve it."*

Erika gulped and looked around for Kari. She was still in the center of the crowd, happy to have been selected to distribute the candy. Taking Lise's hand, Erika approached and stood on the fringes of the crowd. Kari looked right at her and then looked away.

When all of the students had received their sticks, Erika asked quietly, "May I please? For my sister?"

Kari studied Erika for a long moment. Then she smiled sweetly and said, "I'm sorry but they're all gone."

Erika looked down at the basket in Kari's hand. Sure enough, it was empty.

"But—" stammered Erika, "Miss McGrath—she said—she told that all would—"

"She must have miscounted," Kari stated firmly. "There are none left." And she turned and walked away.

Erika looked down at Lise. *"There aren't any left, Lise. I'm sorry."*

Lise stared after Kari. *"She's mean,"* Lise declared. *"I'm going to go tell her mother."*

Lise ran off to find Mrs. Lindstrom. But Erika knew it wouldn't make any difference. Even if Kari was lying about the candy, there was no way to prove it. Erika went to the window and stared out at Silky.

"Oh, Silky," she whispered. "I am afraid that it will always be so."

Tears rolled out of her eyes as she pressed her forehead against the glass. All around her people laughed and talked and celebrated. The room was full of Christmas spirit, but Erika's spirit was broken.

CHAPTER EIGHT

Christmas Eve Rescue

Erika awoke the next morning to sun streaming through her bedroom window. She was groggy with sleep, and for a moment the bright light confused her. She was used to waking up in frosty darkness.

What's going on? she wondered, sitting straight up. Lise was still asleep next to her, curled around her rag doll, peaceful and quiet.

It must be late, Erika thought. *Why didn't Papa or Mama wake me? I'll miss the mail run!*

Erika jumped out of bed, not bothering to dress. She hurried down the narrow staircase and burst downstairs. There sat Mama and Papa, drinking coffee and eating oatmeal.

"What happened?" Erika asked. *"Why didn't you wake me?"*

Mama laughed and looked at Erika in her nightgown. *"It's Christmas Eve day, Erika. No school and no mail today."*

"Yes, of course!" Erika said, shaking her head. "It's Christmas Eve." It had been a long time since she had been allowed to stay in bed so late. She stretched her arms and luxuriated in the feeling of so much sleep.

"No chores today, either?" Erika asked, not really believing she would get off so easily. There were always chores to do.

Mama and Papa looked at each other and smiled. *"You can take the day off,"* Mama said. *"You deserve it."*

"Except for Silky," Papa added. "Horses don't know about Christmas Eve."

Suddenly Erika remembered her most important chore of all. Today was the day she had to return to the Glass Man to pick up the snowball. But how would she do it? What could she tell Papa and Mama to convince them that she needed to take Silky and the wagon and be gone several hours?

Stumped, Erika sat at the long wooden table and looked around. Their small house looked festive and welcoming. Even though there wasn't a lot of money to spare, Mama had decorated the house with Christmas things from Germany, and Papa had brought in a small spruce tree that they would decorate that night.

On the sideboard, Mama's delicious gingerbread, some traditional German cookies, a Christmas fruitcake, and a bowl of oranges waited for tomorrow's feast. Erika longed for one of the spice cookies, called *pfeffernuss* in German, but she knew Mama wouldn't allow it. So she went to the stove to get herself some oatmeal.

Just then, Lise called for Mama and Mama went upstairs. Alone with Papa, Erika decided she would have to confide in him if she wanted to get permission to leave.

"Papa," she said, using German to tell her story faster, *"I need your help. I need to take Silky out today for a special Christmas present for Mama. May I go?"*

"Yes," Papa said. *"But you must take the cutter. Not the wagon."*

"Why?" Erika asked, switching to English.

"A storm is coming."

"What? Look—the sun is shine."

"Shining, you mean. I know, but later it storms. Believe me."

The cutter was a small sleigh with runners instead of wheels. It could glide easily through deep snow, pulled by Silky. Erika wasn't as confident driving the cutter as the wagon, but she was grateful for Papa's cooperation.

Erika hurried to get dressed. A long ride with Silky would be the very best thing to do on her day off.

Papa helped Erika hitch Silky to the cutter, making sure the harness was properly fitted. "Take these warm blankets," he said. "And this," he added, pressing her dinner pail next to her feet. "In case you are hungry."

"Thank you, Papa," Erika said.

Papa waved as Erika called, "Hup!"

Silky heaved forward, and the sleigh took off like a graceful deer. Erika thought Silky looked perfect pulling a sleigh. The contrast of her large, brown body and the slim red wooden sleigh was appealing and comforting. She knew Silky would get them safely to Mr. Dahlberg's and back, no matter the weather or the road.

Halfway to the Glass Man's cottage, near Beaver Creek, Erika saw two figures skiing across an open field of white. Their skis left zigzag patterns in the snow, and their bright knitted caps bobbed as they went along.

"That would be fun," Erika told Silky. *"In Germany I used to ski with my cousins all the time. I wish I had a friend to ski with."*

Silky kept her steady pace, jingling the bells on

the harness. Erika knew the sound of the bells was to warn other horses, but she liked thinking of them as Christmas bells, ringing out holiday greetings to anyone nearby.

Soon Mr. Dahlberg's cottage came into view, and Erika called to Silky to hurry along. She was anxious to get there and see if the Glass Man had been able to fix the snowball. If not, Erika wouldn't have a Christmas gift for Mama.

"Go, Silky, go!" she cried.

Once again Erika stood on Mr. Dahlberg's steps, shivering. The temperature seemed to have dropped in the past hour, and the sky was turning dark.

Papa was right about the storm, Erika thought.

Mr. Dahlberg answered the door wearing a thick sweater and a wool cap. "Ah, there you are!" he said, breaking into a lopsided smile. "I've been waiting for you. The tea kettle is boiling."

Inside, Mr. Dahlberg's house was even more cluttered with glass than before. He cleared a space on a table covered with vases and brought over two tea cups and a glass plate with several kinds of crackers. Erika looked around and tried to find the snowball, but it was nowhere to be seen.

"You have been busy," Erika observed, "making many more things."

"Yes," he answered. "Christmas is my busiest time of year."

Erika sipped the hot, spicy tea and tasted the delicious crackers. It was a welcome rest after the cold drive across Beaver Creek. She was dying to ask about the snowball, but she knew it was more polite to wait until Mr. Dahlberg mentioned it himself.

She felt a bit shy speaking English to him, and he was busy wrapping glass objects in cloth and paper and checking things off on a list. When Erika had finished her tea and carried the cups to the wash barrel, he finally looked up at her.

"Ah," he said. "You've had your tea. So . . . ," he continued, looking here and there, moving things around on a wooden shelf.

For a moment, Erika worried that the snowball was lost.

"Yes, here it is," he finally declared, holding the snowball in both hands. He moved over to Erika and proudly displayed his workmanship. He shook the delicate glass orb, and tiny flecks of paper snow again spun around the miniature town.

"Beautiful!" Erika cried. "As good as new!"

"Ah, good. You are pleased. I am pleased too."

He wrapped the gift in two layers of cloth and another of paper. Then he tied it all up with string.

"Be gentle with this. We don't want it broken again."

"I promise!" Erika said.

Erika buttoned her coat and wound her woolen scarf around her neck. Just as she was leaving, Mr. Dahlberg handed her a small cloth bag with a drawstring. "For you. For your first Christmas in America," he said.

Erika was surprised. She couldn't find the proper English words to thank him. "You are kind and good," she said, hoping he understood.

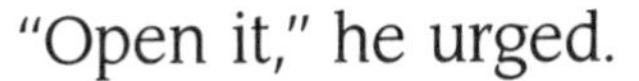

"Open it," he urged.

Erika loosened the drawstring and reached inside. She knew by the feel that it was something small and made of glass. Carefully she pulled it out. "Oh," she breathed, "it is so beautiful!"

She held it toward the lamplight, a small horse made of glass. It looked very much like Silky—the same broad face and strong legs. The same elegant shoulders and even the suggestion of feathers on her legs.

"I made it to look like your horse. I think you are good friends with your horse."

"Yes," Erika agreed, putting the glass horse back into its bag and then into her pocket. "Silky is a good horse. And a good friend."

"A happy Christmas to you, Erika Meyer," he said. "Come and see me again."

"Happy Christmas," Erika repeated. "And thank you many, many times!"

Elated with her horse and snowball, Erika returned to Silky and the cutter. She was stunned at the amount of snow that was falling. A biting wind had kicked up since she went inside. The storm was happening fast.

"We must go," she told Silky.

If Silky hurried, perhaps they would get back to town before the storm worsened and Erika couldn't see to drive.

She tried not to worry, but she had never encountered such a fast-moving storm before. She would have to trust in Silky's ability. Silky had been through quite a few Minnesota winters.

Things went fine until they reached the bridge over Beaver Creek. Here the snow was so thick that Erika could barely see. As the cutter slid over the icy bridge, Erika was sure they would crash right into the creek!

To calm herself, she tried singing. But her teeth were chattering so much she could hardly form the words.

Icy snow pelted her face, and Silky's coat was covered. *We have to get home fast or . . .* Erika could not even allow herself to finish the sentence.

Instead, she thought about Mama and Papa and Lise, safe in their cozy house, the fire going, the tree in the corner waiting to be decorated . . . .

A voice broke Erika's thoughts. *Who could that be?* she wondered. *Who else is out in this storm?* Erika could hardly see her own hands because of the blowing snow. Maybe she had imagined the voice.

"Help!" the voice shouted. "Help! Stop! Please stop!" The voice sounded like a young girl's.

Erika pulled the reins and told Silky to stop. She waited, listening to the voice grow closer, from her right. In the snow she could make out two figures on skis heading toward her. Their caps looked like those of the two skiers Erika had seen on her way to Mr. Dahlberg's.

"Help us!" a girl called. "We're lost!"

"I am right here!" Erika called. She shook Silky's harness so they could hear the bells.

When the skiers approached the cutter, Erika was shocked to see familiar faces. It was Kari and Birgit!

"It's you!" Kari said.

"We're so glad to see you," Birgit added. "I thought we would die out here."

Both girls looked frozen and slightly blue around the lips. Erika knew she needed to get them to shelter fast.

"Leave your skis," she told them. "No room. Climb in. Hurry."

Kari and Birgit kicked off their skis and tumbled into the small sleigh. There wasn't much room, and Erika prayed that Silky had enough energy to pull all of them. She thought fleetingly about the snowball at her feet. Then she realized she couldn't afford to worry about it now.

"Hup!" she cried, slapping the reins. True to her nature, Silky obeyed and took off as though she were freshly rested. *She knows what she has to do,* Erika realized.

But what was there to do? Where would they find shelter if they couldn't make it home? It was too risky to go back over the icy bridge to Mr. Dahlberg's. And the town was still quite far in a storm like this.

"Help me, Silky," Erika whispered. "Help me save us from freezing out here on Christmas Eve!"

The Snowstorm

"Where are we?" Kari shouted to Erika. Her voice could barely be heard in the howling wind. The snow fell so thickly now that Erika could see no further than Silky's ice-coated outline.

"I don't know," Erika admitted, her voice trembling. "There is no way to see."

For all Erika knew, she might have been driving Silky in circles for the past hour. The road had long since disappeared, and no other landmarks were visible.

The girls were so cold that they had almost stopped shivering. Erika knew it was a bad sign when people were so cold that they became still and sleepy.

"My parents will be so worried!" Birgit moaned.

"Mine, too," Kari agreed. "And it's Christmas Eve."

"We should have gone home when it started to snow," Birgit continued.

"We should have brought some food," Kari added.

Erika was grateful for the tea and crackers she had eaten at Mr. Dahlberg's. But regardless of food, they couldn't last long, exposed to the raging storm and biting cold.

We have to find shelter, Erika thought. *Anywhere!*

Silky plodded along without stopping, brave and strong as always.

Kari began to cry, taking deep breaths between her sobs. *I have to do something,* Erika realized. *But what? Singing! That might help the girls—and Silky, too.*

"Silent night, holy night, all is calm, all is bright," Erika sang in a thin voice. To her surprise, Kari and Birgit joined in.

All of a sudden, Silky stumbled and went down on her front right knee. The cutter lurched to a stop.

"Silky!" Erika shouted, lifting herself awkwardly out of the sleigh. "Silky! Are you all right?"

She bent down beside Silky, snow pelting her from all sides. *If Silky is injured and can't go on, then we're truly lost,* Erika thought desperately.

She lifted the horse's leg and ran her hands over it gently. She didn't know much about animal injuries, and she couldn't tell if Silky had strained her leg.

"Can you go on?" she asked Silky, brushing the snow from her horse as best as possible. She took Silky's head in her two hands and looked into her eyes. "Can you make it, girl?" she asked.

Silky whinnied, high and loud, and tossed her head up and down. "Well," Erika said, hugging her horse, "let's go, then. Let's try again."

She told the girls to keep singing as she signaled to Silky to go forward. She tried to keep the reins straight, but suddenly Silky jerked hard to the left.

"What?" Erika asked. "What is wrong?"

Silky continued to turn to the left, so Erika trusted the horse's instincts and followed Silky's lead.

Boom! There was a thudding sound, and the next thing they knew, the cutter had come to a complete stop.

"It's a cabin wall!" Kari shouted.

The girls tumbled out of the sleigh and felt along the snow-covered wall until they found a door. It took all three of them leaning and pushing against the door to open it. As they burst into the small, empty room, Erika realized where they were.

"I cannot believe it," she said, staring. "Our farmhouse. Silky found the way to our old farmhouse!"

"Look, there's firewood by the stove," Kari said.

"We must have left some behind," Erika said.

Kari and Birgit immediately headed for the stove to build a fire.

"I'm taking Silky to the barn," Erika announced, shivering all over again.

Using what strength she had left, Erika unhitched Silky and led her to the barn, which was so familiar and safe that Erika began to cry with relief.

She settled Silky in her stall, covering the horse's icy coat with straw. There was no way to get food or water for Silky. Erika prayed her horse would survive until help came for them.

"How is your leg, hmmm?" she asked, stroking Silky's neck. "You take a sleep and I will come back to see you."

Silky nickered and put her head down, already half asleep.

"You saved our lives," Erika whispered. "Thank you. You are a Christmas angel."

On the way to the house, Erika remembered the dinner pail Papa had packed for her. She felt along the bottom of the sleigh until she found it. She didn't know what was inside, but anything would help. She searched briefly for the snowball, but gave up, fearing it had been kicked out of the sleigh or shattered to bits.

At least we're alive, Erika thought, grabbing the wet lap blankets.

Inside, Kari and Birgit huddled in front of the stove, which glowed with the beginnings of warmth.

"We must take off the wet clothes," Erika said, peeling off her own clothes and spreading them on the bare floor to dry. Dressed only in her woolen underclothes, Erika shivered more than ever.

Kari and Birgit followed her, too cold and tired to talk or disagree. The three of them knelt in front of the stove, grateful for their lives.

Erika thought how strange it was to be in her old house on Christmas Eve with the two people in the world who liked her the least. *Life is strange,* Erika thought. *It takes some very unexpected turns.*

Looking out the small window, it seemed to Erika that the storm was letting up. *Will anyone come looking for us tonight?* Erika wondered. She prayed for the snow and wind to stop, and for Silky to be well.

Then she remembered the dinner pail. She reached for it and showed the others. "My papa sent me with food."

Kari and Birgit seemed to brighten at the thought of food, and they watched hungrily as Erika removed the lid. Inside the pail was bread and cheese, some dried apples, one of the beautiful Christmas oranges, and three of Erika's favorite spice cookies.

Erika spread out the unexpected feast before the girls.

"Thank goodness," Birgit murmured.

"Yum!" was all Kari said. "Shall I peel the orange?"

Erika divided the two pieces of bread and cheese and gave each of them a cookie. Kari carefully sectioned the juicy orange and divided it among them.

They savored every bite, licking the orange juice off their fingers.

"Our Christmas dinner," Erika said, trying to keep her tone light.

"These cookies are the best in the whole world!" Kari declared.

"They are my mama's special Christmas cookies," Erika explained. "Every year in Germany we made hundreds of them."

"My mama makes butter cookies with dried cherries," Birgit said.

"Mine makes molasses cookies dipped in sugar," Kari added.

Soon the three girls were engaged in a lively conversation about their favorite foods and holiday customs, forgetting for a moment that they were stranded in a cold, deserted farmhouse with very little to eat and an injured horse in the barn.

Erika talked easily with them in English, asking now and then for a word she couldn't think of. They laughed at Erika's imitation of her sister, Lise, talking and jumping and twirling around. All of them seemed to forget the tension and bad feelings that had existed before.

When every morsel of food was gone, Kari stood up and went to her coat, which hung on a hook by the door. She rustled around in the pockets for a time and then returned to the stove. She sat down and looked intently at Erika.

"I have a confession to make," she said. She opened her hands, and there was a red and white stick of peppermint. "This was yours from the Christmas festival," Kari said. "I kept it from you. Birgit and I were going to eat it today when we went skiing."

Erika stared at the candy and then at Kari. She didn't know what to say. It was an awful feeling to learn that Kari had purposefully kept it from her.

"It's yours," Kari said, pressing it into Erika's hand. "You saved our lives—and—and it's Christmas. . . . " Kari began to cry, wiping the tears with the back of her hand.

"I have been terrible," she continued. "I've been

mean to you, and I'm very sorry. I know you must hate me and—" Kari put her head down and sobbed harder.

Erika put her hand tentatively on Kari's shoulder. She patted her, much as she did with Silky. "It is—fine," Erika said. "It is over. Don't cry."

Kari straightened up and impulsively grabbed Erika and gave her a hug. Erika was surprised at this, but she hugged Kari back.

"I'm sorry, too," Birgit added. She, too, reached over and joined the hug.

"But can you tell me why?" Erika asked. "I still do not know why you so—hate me?"

Kari shook her head, still drying her tears. "It's hard to explain," she said. "First you beat me at the wagon race. Then it was clear that you were Miss McGrath's favorite, and all the little kids liked you. You're good at math. You have the best singing voice in the whole school. The only thing you couldn't do was speak English."

Erika was silent, trying to digest this information. It was shocking to think that anyone could have been jealous of her when she was so miserable and lonely. But she knew how powerful feelings of jealousy could be. She had been very jealous of Kari and Birgit's friendship.

Erika carefully broke the peppermint into three pieces and handed them out. "Now we are all friends," she said solemnly, and the girls sucked their candy.

Suddenly they heard the sound of horses outside the house and voices calling. Erika ran to the door and threw it open.

"In here!" she called. "Here we are!"

A Christmas to Remember

"Merry Christmas, dear daughter," Mama said to Erika in almost perfect English.

Erika opened her eyes and saw Mama kneeling at the side of her bed.

"What?" she mumbled. "Is it Christmas?"

"It's the middle of Christmas Day. Are you feeling all right?"

"I missed Christmas?" Erika asked. *"It's over?"*

"No," Mama assured her. *"We've been waiting for you to wake up."*

Suddenly Erika remembered the day and night before—the snowstorm, finding Kari and Birgit, being lost, the farmhouse—it all came flooding back.

She remembered Papa and Mr. Lindstrom finding them late at night after the snow had stopped and bringing them home in Mr. Lindstrom's cutter. It had been past midnight when they returned to Silver Lake, and Erika had fallen asleep almost instantly in her warm bed.

"Is Silky all right? Where is she?" Erika asked anxiously. Papa had decided to leave her in the barn at the farmhouse when they left and to return for her later.

"She's in our barn. Papa and Mr. Lindstrom went back for her. Her leg is bandaged. Mr. Lindstrom thinks it's strained, but she'll be fine."

"Poor Silky!" Erika sighed. *"Can I go see her?"*

"Yes," said Mama, *"But first let's have our Christmas. Better late than never."*

They went downstairs, and Erika immediately checked the pocket of her coat. She pulled out the little glass horse and carried it to the spruce tree. Mama and Papa had decorated the tree with dried apples, popcorn strings, and paper butterflies. The tree was also covered with tallow candles waiting to be lit. Lise and Papa sat before the spruce, arranging packages.

"Can we light the candles on the tree?" Erika asked.

"Yes," said Papa, "But I thought we would wait until our guests arrive."

"Guests?" Erika said, confused.

"Kari and Birgit and their parents are coming!" Lise announced. *"And Oskar and the Anderssons and even your teacher. Right, Papa?"*

Papa laughed. "Lise is right. We wanted to celebrate your safe return to us."

Mama nodded and smiled at Erika. *"You were brave in the snowstorm."*

"It was Silky," Erika said. *"She did everything! She was the one who found the farmhouse. We should have a party for Silky!"*

"Time for gifts, first," Papa said, handing Erika two packages.

The first held a wooden checkerboard and checkers, made and painted by Papa. The second was a bead necklace from Mr. Andersson's store.

"I love them. Thank you!" Erika said.

Next, Papa gave Lise her very own wooden hobby horse with a mane and tail made from real horse hair.

"Now I have my very own Silky, too!" Lise exclaimed. She jumped on the toy horse and shouted, "Hup!"

Papa and Mama exchanged practical gifts of clothing and writing paper and spices and cologne. And Erika and Lise presented their own, small gifts to their parents and each other.

The snowball for Mama! Erika suddenly

remembered. Then she felt like crying, realizing she didn't have it. Her special Christmas surprise wouldn't happen.

"Oh! I found something of yours in the cutter," Papa said, interrupting her thoughts. He handed Erika a package wrapped in brown paper.

"Is it—is it the—" Erika couldn't believe it. Could the snowball really have survived the terrible ordeal? She handed it to Mama with wonder. "For you, Mama."

Sure enough, as Mama tore away the paper, the snowball appeared in beautiful, perfect splendor.

Mama was speechless, trying to figure out how Erika could have replaced her prized possession. Tears fell from her eyes as she reached for Erika.

"Don't cry, Mama," Erika said.

"These are happy tears, Erika. I'm so happy—for the gift, and for your safety, and for all we have."

Erika thought it was perhaps the best Christmas her family had ever had. They had survived so much, and they had so much to be grateful for. And so much to hope for in the future.

Just then there was a knock at the door, and Lise ran to open it.

The Lindstroms were there, with the others not far behind. Everyone brought platters of food and gifts to share.

"My goodness!" Mama said.

Soon the house was filled with people. Mr. Andersson played his fiddle, and Mama and Papa filled glasses with cider. Erika and Kari and Birgit had to repeat their Christmas Eve adventure over and over, helping each other add missing details.

"Erika was so brave!" Kari said.

"And she even had food!" said Birgit.

"That was thanks to Papa," Erika explained. "He remembered food."

"And Kari got the stove going," Birgit said.

"And Erika made us sing when we were scared," interrupted Kari.

"But," said Erika, pausing for a moment, "the bravest one of all was Silky."

"Here's to Silky," said Mr. Lindstrom, raising his glass of cider.

"Here, here!" called Papa.

Everyone raised their glasses and saluted the splendid animal who had saved three young girls on Christmas Eve. Kari linked arms with Erika and Birgit, and the three of them made their own Christmas tribute.

"To my best friends—one old and one new!" Kari said, smiling. Erika realized she had rarely seen Kari smile. It was a wonderful, warm smile.

"To my best friends, too," said Birgit. "May we always celebrate Christmas Eve together."

Erika looked around at all the new friends crowded into their small house, eating and drinking, talking and laughing. Erika hadn't thought it would ever happen—that their home would once again be filled with so many caring, familiar faces.

Erika raised her glass and said quietly, "To new friends."

After the girls ate some of the delicious food, Erika said she wanted to go see Silky. She'd been waiting since the moment she opened her eyes.

"I will be back," she said, putting on her coat.

She found the bag of "horse candy" she'd bought for Silky weeks before and slipped outside. She ran for the barn, eager to see her beloved friend.

Silky stood in her stall, keeping the weight off her injured leg. It was bandaged in white cloth from knee to fetlock. It didn't seem to be affecting her appetite, for she was nosing around for the last bits in her feed pail.

"I am sorry you are hurt," Erika said, stroking Silky's soft brown coat.

Silky stopped eating and turned to look at Erika. She nickered energetically, her ears forward and her tail bobbing.

"Merry Christmas, Silky," Erika said, her heart filled with joy. "I hope we'll be together for many Christmases to come!"

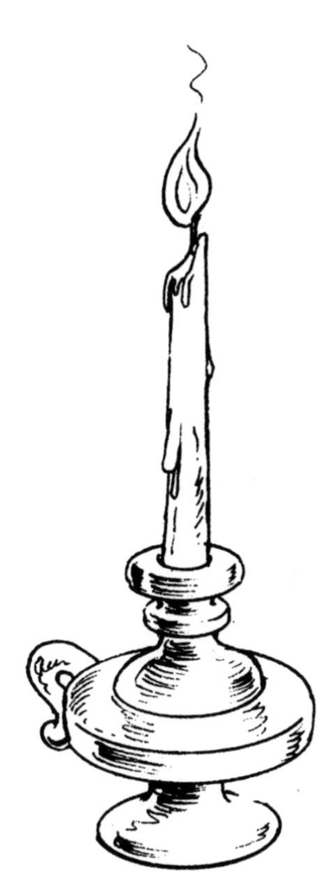

FACTS
ABOUT THE BREED

You probably know a lot about Clydesdales from reading this book. Here are some more interesting facts about this popular draft breed.

∩ An average Clydesdale stands 16.2 hands high, although stallions sometimes grow to more than 17 hands. Instead of using feet and inches, all horses are measured in hands and inches. A hand is equal to four inches.

∩ Clydesdales are usually bay (brown with black mane, tail, and lower leg) or brown. Other common Clydesdale colors include red and blue roan, gray, and black. This breed almost always has heavy white markings on the face and legs.

∩ Clydesdales have long, heavy hair on their lower legs called feathers or feathering. The feathering on a Clydesdale is silky and helps to give the horse its elegant appearance.

∩ The tail of the Clydesdale, like the tail of other heavy breeds, is kept short so that it doesn't get tangled in the reins or harness. Docking, or amputating the tail bone, once a common practice, is now illegal in England and in most of the United States.

∩ The head of the Clydesdale is more refined than the head of other draft or work horse breeds. The profile is usually straight rather than curved.

∩ Clydesdales have well sloped shoulders and prominent withers. The withers of this powerful breed are higher than the croupe, or rear end. This arrangement gives the Clydesdale increased pulling power.

∩ Clydesdales and other draft horses are considered "cold-blooded" horses. Cold-blooded horses, also known as heavy or draft horses, originated in Northern Europe. These horses do not really have cold blood, but they come from cold regions. Hot-blooded horses such as the Arabian come from the hot deserts of Northern Africa. Unlike their hot-blooded relations, cold-blooded horses typically have a calm temperament that, coupled with their large size, makes them well suited for heavy work.

∩ The Clydesdale was developed in the Clyde Valley of Scotland. In the mid-eighteenth century, breeders imported large Flemish stallions to cross with the smaller local draft horses. They also bred their mares with the huge Shires. By the nineteenth century, the Clydesdale breed had emerged.

∩ Scottish immigrants to Canada brought the first Clydesdale to North America around 1850. After the Civil War, Scottish immigrants in the United States began to import Clydesdales. Wisconsin and Michigan became capitals of Clydesdale breeding.

∩ The Clydesdale Horse Society was founded in England in 1877. In 1879, the Clydesdale Breeder's Association of the United States started up. Three years later they published their first stud book. By 1900 the Clydesdale was the third most common draft horse in America.

∩ The Clydesdale has been called a singularly elegant animal among draft horses. Because of their flamboyant style, flashy, spirited bearing, and a high-stepping action, Clydesdales were popular in cities. There they pulled carts full of heavy goods to market.

∩ Today, thanks to the Budweiser™ Clydesdales, this big, elegant horse is probably the most recognized breed of draft horse in the United States.

∩ Clydesdales often pull wagons in teams, consisting of six or eight horses. Each horse in the team has a different job. The pair closest to the wagon are called the wheel horses. When making turns, the wheel horses pull most of the weight of the wagon, so they must be very strong and have great endurance.

∩ The horses at the head of the team are called lead horses. Since they have to cover more ground when taking corners than the rest of the team, they must move quickly.

∩ Swing horses, the pair or pairs in the middle of the team, also must have special skills. Since the swinging pole, which is attached to the wagon, runs between this pair, or pairs, these horses must be especially nimble on their feet so that they do not get hit by the pole when making turns.

∩ Today Clydesdales can be found in Germany, Russia, Japan, South Africa, Australia, and New Zealand, as well as in Canada, Scotland, and the United States.

∩ The most expensive Clydesdale was bought by a Japanese horse lover in 1990 for 20,000 pounds (about 30,000 dollars). The colt that fetched this high price stood a whopping 18.2 hands high!